Spirit Whispers

A Collection of
Ghostly Fairy Tales

Shirl Knobloch

• • •

Spirit Whispers: A Collection of Ghostly Fairy Tales

Edited by: Jennifer Sabatelli

Cover and Artwork by: Shirl Knobloch

ISBN 13: 978-0-692-89061-5

• • •

• • •

"The more enlightened our houses are,
the more their walls ooze ghosts."

-Italo Calvino

Dedicated to all those I have loved in mortal form and continue
to love in spirit.

With special remembrance for my friend Florence, who crossed
during the writing of this book.

• • •

●●●

Table of Contents

• • •

•••

Prologue

I saw my first ghost at about the age of eight. Since then, I have journeyed on a path to explain the world of spirit to others. I live in a historic farmhouse in Gettysburg. Ghosts visit. Most media portrayals of spirits paint them as demons, as malicious entities out to do harm. In reality, the world of spirit is just like ours. There are communities of people, just minus the heaviness of mortal form. Some are bad, but most are good, wanting only to make their presence known in a fleeting mist or shadow across the room...or the placement of a much-missed paw upon a shoulder in the darkness of night.

I hope as you open the pages of my book, the world of spirit opens for you as well. Just because our eyes may not see it doesn't mean it is not there.

Even Naughty Mice Grow Wings

Emily Ann was a very naughty mouse. A very naughty *ghost* mouse, which is one hundred times worse than an ordinary mouse. You see, no one could see Emily Ann. She spent her days and nights misbehaving and having a grand time, sticking her whiskers in freshly-baked cupcakes and dipping her mouse toes in glasses of chocolate milk and then licking her feet!

Emily Ann lived in an old farmhouse with Mr. and Mrs. Hensley. They were old, too, though not as old as their farmhouse, which was very old, two hundred years old. Lots of mice had lived there; some still visited and stole crumbs on Mrs. Hensley's counter. Mrs. Hensley saw them and chased them out the door with her broom. But no one saw Emily Ann. She could do all the bad things she wanted and never got caught.

That is, until Mr. and Mrs. Hensley's granddaughter Marjorie came to live with them. Marjorie's parents had to go to Heaven. Emily Ann didn't know what Heaven was; she knew she was a ghost, but other than that, her life hadn't changed much...except that she was invisible. But not to Marjorie. Marjorie could see her. Emily Ann learned that the hard way when she tried to chew a chocolate chip out of Marjorie's cookie. Marjorie screamed, "Eeek, a mouse!" and Mrs.

Hensley came running with her broom. "Where?" she asked Marjorie. Marjorie pointed to the startled little ghost mouse at the table. Emily Ann dropped the chocolate chip right out of her mouth and screamed, or rather squeaked, too.

Mrs. Hensley scolded Marjorie for making up stories. Later that night, when Marjorie went to sleep, she talked with Mr. Hensley about what happened. "She just needs time, Doris," said Mr. Hensley. "After all, she just lost her mom and dad, she lost her friends back home, and she needs some extra attention," he added. "So she made up a little mouse friend, that's all."

Emily Ann was listening very quietly on the arm of the sofa, waiting for Mr. Hensley's hands to come out of the potato chip bag. Quickly, she stole one. Mr. Hensley was a bit hard of hearing, so he couldn't hear her ghost teeth chewing. Mrs. Hensley shook her head at Mr. Hensley. "I guess you are right, Thomas," she sighed. "Have that talk again with her about Heaven, won't you?" she asked.

There it was again. That word Heaven. Emily Ann felt a twinge that started at the top of her little ghost mouse ears and went all the way down to her tiny ghost mouse toes. The sound of that word seemed to matter, like she was supposed to know this place. But why should she care? She was having so much fun as a ghost mouse, much better fun than the hard life she once lived in the cold, wet fields around the Hensley farmhouse.

Silently, she crept off to sleep, right on top of Mrs. Hensley's yarn basket.   As she drifted off to dreams, Emily Ann wondered why Marjorie could see her.   "Hmmm," she squeaked. "That little girl is going to be a thorn in my mouse side," she cried.   "Now, I will have to make sure she's not around when I go to steal my cookies and cakes in the kitchen."

Emily Ann tiptoed into Marjorie's room at the break of dawn. She crept up beside her pillow and stared at the girl. The tracks of tears lined the little girl's face as she slept. Emily Ann didn't feel mad anymore; instead, she felt her mouse heart fill with a strange sensation. Suddenly, Marjorie opened her eyes. She was just about to let out a blood-curdling scream when Emily Ann squeaked, "Don't scream Marjorie. It's just me, Emily Ann. I am only a mouse, a ghost mouse. You can see me! Would you like to be friends?"

Marjorie's eyes opened like saucers and stared at this fuzzy face, inches from her own. "I don't know," she answered.

"You stink!" Emily Ann sniffed the air with her ghost mouse nose. "You stink, too!" she squeaked at Marjorie. With that, Marjorie let out a giggle and said, "Come on."

She led Emily Ann into the bathroom and filled the tub with bubbles. "Jump in," Marjorie yelled as she climbed into the bathtub. "Mice don't take baths!" Emily Ann squeaked. "Well, you do if you want to be my friend and put your stinky face on my pillow," Marjorie answered. Emily Ann gingerly placed a mouse toe onto a yellow duck floating in the tub. "Come on, all stinky parts in," said Marjorie, and she placed Emily Ann in the water beside her. "I won't let go," she told the little ghost mouse as she held on to her fur. "Now scrub!!"

Emily Ann scrubbed her mouse feet, her mouse ears, and her mouse tummy. She wiped the soap off her mouse whiskers and stood at the edge of the tub, using Marjorie's washcloth as a bath towel. "Come on," said Marjorie. "It's time for breakfast."

Marjorie didn't say a word about Emily Ann, though she snickered about her bad table manners. "We are going to have a talk about this later," she told the ghost. "What's that, Marjorie? Did you say something?" asked her grandpa.

• • •

Marjorie shook her head and gazed at Emily Ann's feet, which were now in the butter dish. *Well, at least they are clean*, she thought to herself.

Emily Ann was having a grand time hanging off the side of Mrs. Hensley's teacup when Marjorie said, "May I be excused?" Then, she grabbed the naughty mouse's paw and whisked her through the air, carrying her off to her room. "Emily Ann, you have to stop being naughty!" she scolded. "You can't just chew a person's cookie or sit in their butter dish. It's not polite. You have to learn manners; I am going to teach you."

"Manners!" Emily Ann squeaked. Her whiskers curled up in a bow. "I don't want to learn manners. I like being naughty," she cried. Marjorie retorted, "Not if you are going to be my friend. You can share my cookies, just don't put your mouth on them. You can share all my stuff, just don't be stinky and mouse them up with your mouse smell! You will be a well-behaved little mouse from now on."

And so, Emily Ann learned. She learned proper table manners. She took morning baths with Marjorie and tried to wash off as much of her mouse smell as possible. She combed her whiskers with Marjorie's toothbrush...even good mice have some naughty habits. And that summer, the two became best friends. Mrs. Hensley was happy that Marjorie's mood brightened. Mr. Hensley was glad that his potato chip bags seemed to last longer.

Mornings were spent in the garden, saying hello to the morning glory faces as they opened to the sun. Evenings were firefly catching times, with Emily Ann's sharp mouse eyes finding their little lights in the dark. On those nights, Emily Ann took a sponge bath in the sink, since mice apparently find rolling in stinky garden stuff irresistible.

The two friends were inseparable. Comments about Marjorie's constant giggling and imaginary friends wafted through the farmhouse. "At least she is happy," sighed Grandpa Hensley. "So what if she has imaginary playmates?"

Marjorie would often read fairy tales to Emily Ann about evil queens and stepmothers. "They were naughty because nobody taught them to be nice," Emily Ann whispered. "They didn't have a best friend like me." Then she added, "Will we always be best friends, Marjorie?" "Always, Emily Ann," said Marjorie. "Pinkie to paw swear always."

One afternoon, while crossing the farm fields, Marjorie asked, "How did you die, Emily Ann?" "I...I...I don't remember," stuttered the little mouse. Marjorie saw how frightened Emily Ann became when they walked by the cornfield. The little ghost always crept inside Marjorie's overalls to hide.

One morning, as the sun came up, Emily Ann felt something weird on her back. It sort of tickled and felt very warm. "Marjorie, Marjorie, wake up!" she squeaked. Marjorie opened her eyes; they looked as big as they did the first time Emily Ann woke her, that first morning in her bed. "Emily Ann, you have wings!!!" Marjorie cried. Emily Ann crept over to the floor length mirror on Marjorie's door. Then, she saw them. Glistening white wings, so beautiful in the morning sunlight, fluttered on her little mouse shoulders.

Then a sad feeling came over her tiny ghost mouse heart. She seemed to know what they meant. "Good mice go to Heaven, Marjorie," she squeaked. "No, I don't want you to go! Stay here, be a naughty mouse again, stink up my room! I don't care, just don't go!!!" Tears rolled down Marjorie's face. Emily Ann touched them with her tiny paw and wiped them away. "I have to go, Marjorie. My family is waiting for me. Your family waits there, too. One day you will see them again...and me, too!"

"I remember now, Marjorie," said Emily Ann. "It was in the cornfield. I was sleeping when the big tractor..." Emily Ann's eyes filled with tears. "It's okay," said Marjorie. "My parents saw a big truck, too..."

Suddenly, a beautiful sunbeam shot through the lace curtains and landed on the little ghost mouse's head. She kissed Marjorie good-bye and vanished in the beam. Marjorie walked into the bathroom and held her toothbrush to her chest. Right before she left, Emily Ann apologized for having used Marjorie's toothbrush as a whisker brush. "That's okay, Emily Ann," she cried. "Even naughty mice grow wings...pinkie to paw swear."

His Eye Is On the Sparrow

Terry Larkin stared wistfully out her window this sunny, spring day. *One more day until my wedding*, she thought to herself. "I wish you could have been here, Grandpa. You would love Jeff." Smiling, she whispered, "Grandpa, his name is Sparrow. Can you believe that?" With a laugh, she added, "Yes, I guess you know...you probably planned the whole thing!"

Then, her smile turned to sadness as she watched the tiny sparrows at her birdfeeder, realizing that her grandpa wouldn't be there to see her walk down the aisle. Her wedding invitations told guests to throw birdseed, not rice. Grandpa would have liked that. *Rice swells in their bellies; it harms them. Always throw birdseed at a wedding.* Grandpa would smile that she remembered.

When she was a child, she spent many afternoons feeding the sparrows. They were her grandpa's favorite. He always told her they were the most beautiful of beings. "Birdwatchers have traveled the world to see birds of paradise and blue bower birds and such. Didn't they know how beautiful the sparrows were, not the drab brown birds that everyone treats as *ordinary*?" he would tell her. "God knows how special they are. His eye is on them," he would add with a wink in his own eye.

Terry never forgot those last words of her grandfather. "Just like the sparrow, my eyes will be on you, even though you cannot see me." With that, he closed his own eyes.

That was eight years ago. Terry had changed so much in those years, gone to college, started a job at the University library, and met Jeff. His library card said *Jeff Sparrow.* When she looked down at it, she smiled. "That's a pretty smile you have," he said. "It's your name," she said. "My name?" he asked. "Yes, sparrow, my favorite bird." "When is your break? Would you like to get some coffee?" he smiled. "Favorite bird," he laughed. "I would have said *lark,* Miss Terry Larkin," reading her name tag. "No, sparrow," she added.

And so it began. Terry knew he was the one, right after he threw his doughnut crumbs to the tiny sparrows on the library lawn. And now, one year later, they were starting their life together as Mr. and Mrs. Sparrow tomorrow.

"I'd best get some packing done," she murmured to herself. Jeff and she were off on a bird watching trip to the Amazon. *The Lark and the Sparrow*--that's what their friends called them. Shower gifts were emblazoned with birds...bird towels, bird dishes, bird bedspreads. It became a standing joke that they would be living in their own little birdhouse.

Terry awoke to the sunshine. The sparrows were chirping at the feeder. "I will see you guys soon," she whispered at the window. "I have a wedding to get ready for." She was the most beautiful of brides. If ever a sparrow's heart sang, it was Jeff's the moment he saw her walk down the church aisle. Guests had all been handed their little satin pouches of birdseed for the wedding toss. Two hundred sixteen guests... the couple was blessed with so many family and friends.

As Terry reached the altar and stood beside her groom, the priest said a few words to the congregation. "Family and friends, we have an unexpected visitor this morning. Don't be alarmed—somehow, a tiny sparrow chose to join our wedding this morning. He is up high. We will leave the church doors open so he finds his way back outside. I just wanted to let you know in case he should choose to swoop down during the ceremony." Terry's eyes filled with tears. *Two hundred seventeen guests,* she whispered quietly.

***Note: Spirits often visit in the form of animals, many times birds.

Buried Hurts

Hurtful memories haunt the mind more powerfully than any ghost. And so it was for Josh, a peasant farmer's son who lived on a small patch of tenant land, about 10 miles from the king's castle.

About eight years earlier, a ghost of a memory came to live in Josh's mind and heart. It was freezing cold; the wind was howling, and a blinding snowstorm was shrouding what little light the moon cast upon his father's field. Josh and his dad were out collecting whatever scraps of firewood they could find to warm the night. At first, they thought she was a wolf, this large, dark shadow in the snow. "Run inside, get my gun!" his father shouted. "No!" said Josh, struggling in the deep snow to get a closer look at this being. "She is a dog, Father," he cried. "She needs our help."

With those words, Josh lumbered in the drifts and came close to her side. Her long legs were trembling; she was soaked to the bone and shivering. With deep, sorrowful eyes, she looked at the boy. He held out his hand to her, and she placed her snout into his palm. Josh's father carried the hound inside the farmhouse and placed her at the dwindling fire. The boy ran to his bed, gathered up his tattered blanket, and wrapped it around her shivering body. They offered her a sip of broth, but she hardly had the strength to lift her tired head.

"She is too far gone, son. Don't get your heart and hopes up high. Besides, we can hardly feed the two of us now, can we?" his father asked. "Come to bed now, get some rest. Let her be in peace."

Josh laid his body down beside the dog and slept away what remained of the night. When he awoke, she lay very still. Josh's tears fell upon her fur. "She is gone, son. Come along, let us find a place to bury her in this frozen earth."

The ground was so hard, Josh's father managed to dig only a very shallow grave. It would have to do. Before they placed her inside, Josh took the lovely brocade collar off her neck. "You must have been loved by someone dearly to have such a special collar," Josh whispered to himself. "Perhaps one day I shall meet them and tell them where you rest." Together, father and son laid her down into the icy ground. Josh labored all day in the cold, gathering large rocks to build a memorial cairn on top of her grave. If one thing was abundant on their barren patch of land, it was rocks.

When the storm had finally passed and warmer temperatures melted some of the snow, Josh and his dad heard the sound of horses on the road to their farmhouse. Grand horses, about ten of them, led in procession by a beautiful white stallion, all flying the colors of the king. They swiftly approached the farmhouse door, and Josh's father opened to see the prince standing in his doorway!

"I am looking for my Brigit," the prince said. "She is my wolfhound, my loyal companion. She was blinded by the snow the other evening and became lost in the storm. Have you seen her?" he asked with pleading eyes. Josh's eyes grew large as saucers, and his mouth was ready to open when his father took his arm and told him to go get some tea for the prince. "No, we have not seen such a dog," Josh's father answered. "Isn't that right, Josh?" he called to the boy. "We have not seen her." Josh faintly whispered, "Yes, Father."

The prince put on his gloves, waving away the tea cup. "I have no time for tea; I must keep searching." With that, he opened the door, climbed on his horse, and rode off with his men.

When he was sure they were alone once more, Josh muttered, "Papa, why?" "Hush, child," his father replied, "we will not speak of this again. The prince would have blamed us for killing her. The king would have thrown us in the castle dungeon, and we would be dead now, too. Never tell a soul what happened here, do you understand me?" The small boy bowed his head in reply.

• • •

Years passed, and he never told a soul. But the hurt lay buried in his heart. You see, the spring before, he had let his cat out for the night and never saw him again. He spent days calling for him, nights staring out his window across the dark field, wondering where he was. If truth be told, he never really stopped searching, always hoping to see a tiny fluff of grey fur on the horizon, running towards him. He knew the hurt of not knowing. And now the prince carried that hurt as well. Father told him that the king could afford to have hundreds of wolfhounds; losing one would not matter. But Josh knew each one *mattered*, and it weighed heavily upon his heart.

Things had gotten worse for the father and son. Debts had piled up, like the cairn of rocks the boy had made. His father's health weakened, and on a brisk, winter day, he took to his bed and never awakened. The king's collector came to the door a few days later; tax payment on the farm was past due. By now, the elderly king had passed on, as well; the young prince had replaced him on the throne. "I have no payment," Josh told the collector. "Then you must come with me to debtor's prison," the man said, grabbing Josh's arm forcefully.

When they reached the castle walls, Josh saw a large crowd gathered, watching a progress of horses and carriages as it passed by. Something stirred inside Josh's heart. "I must speak to the king!" he cried. "You fool, what would you have to tell his Majesty?" the collector humorously exclaimed. "I have something important to show him!" With that, he broke free of the collector's grasp and ran to the front of the crowd.

"I have Brigit's collar!" he screamed, reaching into a tattered pouch in his coat pocket. There was a roar of applause and cheers. The young king could barely hear this poor peasant, but he saw him waving something in the air above his head. "That man, what is he waving?" he asked his servant. "Bring him to me now!"

Josh placed the collar in the king's hand. He told him the memory of that snowy night, of Brigit and her passing. The king responded with only three short words—"Let him go!"

Josh walked home. That night, in the moonlight, the sound of a horse's hooves startled his sleep. He looked out his window and saw a shadowy figure climb down from a handsome white stallion and walk to the edge of his farm field. The figure knelt at the base of the rock cairn and buried his face in his hands. He stayed there for long time, then mounted his horse and rode off into the night.

In the morning, Josh walked out to Brigit's grave. There, lying on the rocks, was her beautiful brocade collar, and tied within it was a roll of parchment. Josh unrolled the paper and read these words:

> *DEED, this parcel of land paid in full, signed King William. With one condition, the grave of loyal Brigit never be disturbed.*

And it never was. To this day, if you walk upon a field in the harsh countryside, you might happen upon a cairn of rocks. Local villagers will tell you never to disturb it, for fear of fairy folk. And perhaps the fairy folk do tend the grave of one very loyal wolfhound, to this very day.

THE GIRAFFE AND THE DOVE

In a lush forest on the African plain lived a beautiful giraffe. Except for the trees, she was the tallest of beings and had only one friend, a tiny grey dove. Each day, the giraffe sought out the freshest leaves upon which to snack. Each day, the dove sought out the giraffe, for she had stolen his tiny heart.

How is that possible, you might say? How could a tiny dove lose his heart to a giant of a giraffe? The ways of love are seldom easily explained. Perhaps it was her first hello to him as he perched in the tall branches. From that moment on, his tiny dove heart beat for her and her alone. Each day, he cooed in her ear. Each night, his mourning calls lulled her to sleep under the tall trees. The dove watched her gaze upon the stars. *"How beautiful,"* she would whisper. *"If only I could hold such lovely light."*

The dove would do anything for his giraffe friend. His brave heart set upon a quest. *I will capture one for her.* Each night, he flew up in the night sky, soaring higher and higher, trying to catch a star for his love.

But it was never high enough. The dove grew more and more exhausted, trying to catch a star for his giraffe. Some days, he was too tired to coo. The giraffe broke off tender leaves to line his nest, never knowing how he spent his nights under the moon and stars.

This continued for some time. The faithful dove waiting for his mate to close her long-lashed eyes and setting out upon his nightly quest, under the starry skies. His wings and heart beat rapidly as he flew higher and higher in the sky, but alas, he could not reach the stars.

And so he wept...his mournful coos filled the night sky as he soared above. The dove's wailings set the jungle creatures stirring, and his love opened her eyes and gazed upward. A trail of blazing light crossed the night sky as a falling star fell to earth.

"Dove, dove, wake up...we must go find it!" the giraffe cried. But the dove's nest was empty.

The giraffe set out to follow where the light had fallen. It was not far, just within a patch of trees to the north side of the river. She walked, calling to her dove friend to follow, but he didn't answer. Soon, she came to the patch of trees and searched upon the ground.

In the faint moonlight, she came upon a sorrow. There lay her friend, his eyes closed and his wings spread widely apart, as if in flight. Sadly, she laid her tall neck down and kissed his beak, never knowing the brightest light she sought was right beside her in the trees all along, the light of a little dove's beating heart.

Addeline's Friend

Addeline lived alone in a stately Victorian home on the outskirts of the city. She was eighty-seven years old and had lived in the house all her life. Born in the same bedroom where she now lay ill, it seemed her first breath and her last would be taken under the same roof.

Addie had married a hometown boy and raised three children here. They all scattered, as children do. Two boys were living in New York, her daughter out west, and Addie's husband gone twelve years now. She didn't mind living on her own. Ever since she was a little girl, her books were her friends. She kept to herself, a shy child, the kind adults whispered about with over imaginations.

Addie had a childhood friend, Emmie. She investigated all the nooks of the Victorian home with her and all the corners of secret garden paths only the two of them knew. Addie saw Emmie until the summer she turned eleven. Then, Emmie didn't come around anymore, a relief to her parents who never understood this figment of their daughter's creative mind. "Too many books, no friends," her father would say. "She needs to get out more. She spends too much time in her room and in this house." What a relief when Addie stopped mentioning her.

But Addie never forgot. When her own children were little, she told them stories of her friend, how they sat under the blossoming cherry tree in the yard for hours, just feeling the warm sunlight and watching ladybugs in the grass. Soon, though, her children grew older and didn't believe her anymore. They were tired of their mother's strange memories; they needed memories and friends of their own.

Addie focused on her gardens, her books, and her paintings; her world became quieter and smaller as the decades passed. Now, she spent her days alone, except for the caregiver who stopped in for an hour or two twice a day to make sure she was fed and comfortable.

Addie's daughter was first to receive the call. "Mrs. Norris, it's your mother. She is fading in and out or reality. She keeps mentioning Emmie. Do you know who she is talking of?" "Don't worry," she told the caregiver, "Mom always was a bit eccentric. Now I guess she has totally gone over the edge. Just keep her comfortable. I have two big meetings this week, but I will be out there as soon as I can."

Addie drifted deeper and deeper into lengthy sleep, only stirring for short periods of time, always calling for Emmie. She would point her fingers to the window and say, "Look, she has come back! I always knew she would." Then, she would drift back into her silent world of sleep again.

One morning, the caregiver came to find her sprawled across the bedroom floor. "She was calling me to follow," Addie said. Helping her back to bed, the worried caregiver again phoned her daughter. "I don't think she should be home anymore," she said. "Just do the best you can. I don't have time for this right now!" an angry voice answered.

Days passed. Addie was hardly swallowing a few sips of broth now, but she seemed to possess an air of tranquility about her. "She's here, you know, waiting," Addie whispered. "Just lie down and rest, Miss Addie," the woman said, shifting the pillows beneath her head. Then, the caregiver left Addie for the rest of the afternoon. At nighttime, she checked back in on her. Again, she saw the woman sprawled on the floor, this time, her body cold and unresponsive. "Oh, Miss Addie, I am so sorry you had to die alone."

The sorrowful woman didn't hear the soft voice answer from the corner of the room. "But I didn't. Emmie came. I told you she would!"

The two spirits drifted down into the garden. Emmie shouted, "C'mon, I'll race you to the cherry tree!" "Emmie, I'm too old to race," Addie whispered back. "Anyway, that old cherry tree died decades ago," she added wistfully. Smiling, Emmie shouted, "Just look!" With that, Addie glanced down at her two youthful legs, white anklet stockings tucked into black and white saddle shoes. She was running, racing at full speed toward the corner of the garden where the two of them sat on so many sunny summer days. Suddenly, she felt the sunlight on her hair, long and braided now. Then, Addie saw her. The old cherry tree was in full blossom. In the distance, a young boy appeared, running towards them. He seemed familiar; he reminded her of her husband, a long time ago, when boyhood features had not totally left his youthful face.

Mrs. Norris arrived a few days later, her two brothers soon after. They met with the family lawyer who read Addie's instructions in her will. "She is leaving the Victorian to the town historical society, with provisions for them to keep the gardens blooming." "No way!!" shouted one of her sons. "I always knew she was loony," the other said, "always talking of ghosts and spirits in the house." "We could have sold this place to a developer for millions," their sister sighed. "Now, some old people in town will hold teas here, chat about the ugly paintings, and walk among some old dying trees."

● ● ●

Yes, teas *were* held in the garden. The horticultural society fertilized and weeded and brought new life to the withering boughs and blossoms. And always, in one special corner, a trio of friends sat, smiling in the sunlight, watching ladybugs crawl by in the grass.

At night, while the house was quiet, friends roamed about, enjoying the nooks and corners and strolling by the paintings, being very careful not to disturb a thing. Sometimes, passersby would swear they saw a fleeting shadow float by one of the windows, but it must have only been their overactive imaginations...don't you think?

GHOSTS IN THE SNOW

Miriam was a photographer. She loved to take pictures in the cemetery; the beautiful angel statues to her were the loveliest of subjects, especially in the snow. Miriam loved the cemetery snow, when all the world was as silent as those now at rest, when ice crystals formed caps and shawls around the shoulders of angels and saints.

One December afternoon, while flakes still fell to the ground, Miriam drove to her local cemetery and started taking photos. Snowflakes look beautiful on film, like spirit orbs drifting in the air. Trees in snow took on beauty unlike any other time of the year. Miriam loved the trees; they called to her and her camera, as if a snow spirit hid inside each one.

In one tree, a dove sat perched on a snowy branch. It cooed relentlessly. Miriam answered. "What is it you wish, little one? Do you wish your picture taken on this snowy day?" With that, Miriam snapped her camera. Looking through the lens, Miriam saw a shadowy mist beside the dove in one of the photos. Probably just moisture in the air, she noted to herself.

The dove followed as she walked through the grounds, perching on a nearby tree each time she stopped to take more photos. He cooed and cooed, mournfully, as if trying to tell her something of great importance. Miriam began snapping more photos; again, this strange mist appeared next to him. "Now, that is odd," she thought to herself.

Her hands were becoming numb from the cold. Realizing it was time to start heading back to the warmth of her car, Miriam paused to take one last photo of her friend in the tree. But he wasn't there. "I guess you flew home, too," she said to herself.

Much to her surprise, as Miriam turned to go back to her car, the dove flew overhead, his wings whistling in the brisk air. He turned around and around again, repeatedly flying over Miriam's head, then flying off and back again. Miriam decided to follow. Soon, they came to a statue of St. Francis. "How beautiful," Miriam sighed. St. Francis was partially shrouded in snow. One of his hands held a stone dove. Then, Miriam glanced at the ground. Beside St. Francis' feet, there lay a grey dove, almost totally covered in snow. Above her, the other dove had landed on top of St. Francis' head, cooing loudly.

"Oh," she cried. Gently, Miriam picked up the tiny body. The ground was frozen solid; there was no way to bury her there.

• • •

"I will take care of her," she told the little dove, staring down at the cold body of his little mate.

She carried the dove to her car, placed her in a blanket, and slowly drove the short distance home. Miriam took a large bag of potting soil out from her garage shelf and filled a beautiful flowerpot. She placed the dove inside and covered her with soil. "There," she whispered. "When the ground thaws, I will put you in my garden, right beneath my own statue of St. Francis."

Miriam took the flowerpot, opened her garage door, and went out into the garden. As she placed the pot down in the snow, she heard a whistling of wings in the tree overhead. Above her sat the dove from the cemetery. Not realizing until now that she still had her camera around her neck, Miriam once again snapped a photo of him. Once, again, the mist occurred. "I see you have found her again," she smiled.

Miriam kept her promise, and when spring arrived, she buried the little dove's remains. Her mate lingered in Miriam's garden for several more years, always perching in the tree above St. Francis' head until one day, Miriam found him lying still beside the statue. Miriam placed him in the ground beside his mate.

On snowy days, Miriam still takes photos of the trees in her yard. In some of them, two misty forms seem to materialize among the branches. Friends say it's just moisture in the air when Miriam shows them the photographs, but Miriam knows the photos reveal so much more than most eyes think they see.

Ranger and Stormy

acob Sanders and his wife, Jean, live in a small cottage in a rural area of Tennessee. They own about thirty acres, twenty of which are undeveloped woodlands. Not many pass through this backwoods part of the country; the closest road is the interstate, about two miles to the north.

It happened almost fifteen years ago. Jean and Jacob had been living there for only about six months. On a very stormy evening, a tiny visitor disturbed their sleep. They were accustomed to the sounds of the forest and the raccoons and possums and foxes that sometimes came a bit too close to their property in search of a meal. But this was different; they heard high pitched yelps and scratching at their screen door. "Go to sleep, Jean," her husband said, hoping that whatever it was, coon, possum, or skunk, would just tire and run away.

But the yelps continued, plaintive cries for help and scratching that grew more intense and frantic as the minutes passed. Jacob got out of bed and turned on the outside light. There stood a wet, bedraggled little white dog, paws in the air, begging for help. "My, what have we here?" Jacob asked, scooping him up in his arms. "Jean, we have a guest."

Jean's sleepy eyes watched as the tiny dog shook the rain off his body and ran frantically back to the screen door. "I think he wants back out," she said. "No," Jacob answered. "I think he wants us to go outside with him."

The couple watched as the little dog paced back and forth, barking at their feet and clawing at the screen. The tiny bell on his blue collar jingled as he ran back and forth. "You wait here, Jean. I am going outside." "I'm coming too!" Jean answered, fearful of what the darkness hid from her young husband.

Together, they grabbed their coats and boots and Jacob's flashlight and followed the tiny dog. It was hard to keep up with him; he set off in a determined pace as soon as they opened the door. "Something is wrong," Jean said. "I just feel it." "He is headed for the interstate. Maybe someone is stuck on the road and needs help," Jacob answered. They walked the two miles north of their home, watching as the tiny dog stopped, waited for them to follow, and then set off again.

They came to a deep ravine off the road where the tiny dog sat, waiting. Shining his flashlight, Jacob could see deep skid marks in the mud. "This doesn't look good, Jean. Go home and call for help!" he shouted. Handing her the flashlight, he added, "I am just going to wait here. Don't worry. It's too dark and slippery. I cannot get down there."

Jean didn't believe her husband. She knew that the moment she left for home, he would be trying to climb down that ravine. There was no discussion about it, he was staying. "Hurry!" he shouted. "Someone may still need help down there." Reluctantly, Jean left.

The tiny dog followed her. She was grateful for his help along the path on this dark night. When she reached her cottage, she phoned the State Police. Then, she and her tiny companion set off again in the night.

The troopers had already arrived when the pair reached them. Jean's eyes searched for Jacob, but she knew in her heart where he would be. And sure enough, the troopers told her what he had found. An older woman had gone off the road in the storm. "There was nothing we could do. She must have died instantly." Jacob now climbed back up the ravine slowly, gripping onto branches and vines as he struggled to get back to his wife's side. His face was white; Jean's flashlight beam illuminated a look in his eyes unlike any she had even seen before.

"Where's the dog?" he asked with a frantic tone in his voice. "He...he was just here a minute ago. Oh no, I hope he isn't lost again!" Jean cried. "No, Jean...not lost," Jacob answered in a hushed voice.

"Jean, there was a woman in the car. She was dead. In the back seat was a large, black dog. He was gone, too. I watched as the troopers lifted them out of the car. Under him was a tiny white dog. I saw him, Jean. He had a blue collar with a bell on it. They were dead, Jean, all three of them."

Jean saw Jacob's hands trembling. She reached out to put her arms around his soaked body. "Did you tell anyone?" she asked. "No," he answered. "They would think I had one too many tonight," he sighed. "Or maybe that I was crazy," he continued. "Let's just go home, Jean. I'm so tired."

The next morning, Jean called the State Police. They had located the woman's family, who lived three states away. "What about the dogs?" she asked. "Oh, the family doesn't want them. We are bringing the remains to be destroyed," replied the trooper, a bit surprised she would ask about them. "Could we take them?" she pleaded. "We have so much land. Could we lay them to rest in the woods behind our cottage?" The trooper hesitated, knowing this went against protocol for these situations. But, he was a dog lover and finally answered "Yes." Jacob went to pick up the two friends in his pickup and brought them back home. "The trooper says they were best friends. The big one was Ranger, the little one, Stormy. How about that? Stormy...quite fitting, don't you think?" Jacob laughed nervously, as he clutched the tiny, still body in his arms. "You're a good boy, such a very good dog," he sighed as he patted the little one's head. As he lifted Ranger in his arms, he spoke to him, as well. "You have a very good friend," he whispered. "Take care of him now."

The couple placed Ranger and Stormy in a grave, side by side. That was fifteen years ago, but they never forgot. They never stop clearing and tending the space where they lay together, always placing wildflowers above. Sometimes, Jean leaves little treats for both of them, a home baked cookie or a tiny dish of leftovers. Jacob tells her the coons and possums sure enjoy these snacks, but something in his heart hopes a tiny white dog and big black one enjoy them, too.

On stormy nights, Jacob sometimes hears a high-pitched yelping and scratching on their screen. He never mentions this to Jean; he lets her sleep. But Jean isn't sleeping. She is listening, too, for those familiar sounds in the storm. The sounds of a tiny little dog, seeking help for his two best friends.

• • •

THE RUSTLE OF GHOSTS

*L*ucy sat at her dining room table. The realtor had politely *asked* her to leave during the open house, but Lucy wasn't having any part of that. This was her home; she would see who wandered about her rooms, wandered through her memories. It was her home and her choice as to whom it would be sold.

She had been there about forty years now, never married. She bought the small ranch home when the development was only a few years old. The previous homeowner had gotten a job transfer out of state. It was a nice starter home, clean, in good shape, perfect for a single woman who didn't have the knowledge or finances to take on expensive home repairs.

Lucy was a sensitive soul; she could sense energy in places. She had been to a few run-down homes for sale with rooms full of ghosts, full of baggage from those who had lived and died there.   This home on Grand Oaks Drive was different...clean. "No ghosts," she whispered to herself when she found it.

Then she walked into the backyard.   It was a spacious property. Lucy loved that. She loved to garden, loved the idea of welcoming birds and butterflies and bees to her home. The real estate agent left her alone to walk the property for a few moments, and Lucy could feel the rustle of large oaks around her. But there were none on this land. None in the entire development for that matter. Oh, homeowners had planted some small, ornamental trees—dogwoods, cherry blossoms, and such—but no tall, stately trees watched over this street or the surrounding ones. Lucy could feel them, the ghosts of tall oaks. Sad that this street still possessed the name, but none for which that name was chosen.

Lucy was saddened by this. She loved trees. She talked to them, always wanted a home surrounded by them. Strange, she could *feel* them. It was if they were talking to her, the spirits of those long gone from this patch of earth.

Forty years...now, Lucy looked out her dining room window and saw the leaves of tall oaks rustling in the breeze. She remembered the day she drove to the park and collected her bags of acorns. She planted them, all of them, for she knew some would be claimed by foraging beings. Soon, the heads of tiny oaks appeared, and tiny saplings grew. And forty years later, tall oaks stretched their limbs to the sky.

When friends drove up to visit, the first thing they would say was, "That must be Lucy's house, the one surrounded by trees." And they were right. From the bottom of the hill, one could see across the sky until the crest and the yellow house, when tall oaks obstructed the view.

Forty years...her trees were still strong, but she was not. Arthritis had weakened her joints. Just getting to the store zapped all her strength. She didn't want to leave this place, but she realized it was time. Her younger sister just bought a townhouse in a retirement community, and the unit next door was available. "Does it have a garden?" Lucy asked. "A small patch, enough for a rose bush or two," her sister answered on the phone. Lucy sighed, afraid to ask the next question. "How about trees, are there trees?" "Yes, there is a big oak in front of my sidewalk. We can share him," Lucy's sister answered with a laugh in her voice.

And so the realtor was called. The open house was scheduled. Young business couples wandered through the rooms. *It has potential,* they whispered. *Needs some landscaping, maybe an in-ground pool out back. We can expand the back and make a great room if we chop down some of those trees.*

Lucy cringed. Her worst fear, the destruction of her trees. Suddenly, a young couple with a baby walked in the front door. The husband tried to shush his wife. "Be quiet, never let them know you love the place." "I can't help it," she said.

"Did you see all those trees? So beautiful. Think what a great treehouse we can build for Joey."

Lucy turned to the young woman. "You like trees?" she asked. The young woman blushed with embarrassment, "You will probably think me crazy, but I talk to them," she answered, her voice filled with hesitancy. "No, I don't think you are crazy," Lucy answered.

The young couple walked outside and contemplated a future among the oaks. The realtor sat down beside Lucy. "Usually, we wait until the open house has ended," she told Lucy. "But we have a few very good buyers here. So far, three strong offers, and one questionable one from a young couple struggling to get a mortgage."

"It's theirs," said Lucy. "I have to strongly offer advice to not choose that offer," the realtor said. "I already took my advice, from the trees," Lucy answered.

The Realtor shook her head, collected her open house flyers, and briskly walked out the front door, mumbling to herself something about a stupid old woman.
Two months later, a young father started on that tree house for his son as his wife placed a birdhouse among a patch of

newly planted wildflower seeds. The oaks rustled in the breeze, sighing with contentment. "You know," called the young mother, "it sounds like so many oaks, like a whole forest of oaks rustling behind us." "You and your trees," the husband laughed.

HoMe

Janie and Ethan had just bought into the American dream—their first home. Albeit, it was small, but there was time for additions and renovations as needed. For now, the two-bedroom blue bungalow was perfect. That is, except for the barking dog whose high-pitched yelps kept waking them up at night. Woken from slumber, Ethan would turn on the porch light and look outside. Nothing. He would go back to bed, almost caught in sleep once more, when the canine cries began again.

"Ask the neighbors, Janie," he said at the breakfast table. "We have to find out whose dog this is."

Janie was shy; she wasn't one to strike up conversations with strangers, and there were only two other houses on the street. One was boarded up...*no dogs there*, she thought. Which left the green ranch across the street. It looked *friendly* enough. She worked up her confidence and decided to ring the doorbell after Ethan left for work.

Janie walked up the front path surrounded by little yellow marigolds. There was a welcome sign with two calico cats across it. "That's comforting," she sighed. Suddenly, before she reached the stair landing, an elderly woman opened the door with a smile.

"Hello," she said, her wrinkled eyes crinkling up at the edges. "I'm your new neighbor," Janie answered softly. "What's that?" the woman asked. "I am hard of hearing. You have to speak louder."

Taking a deep breath, Janie spoke again, this time louder. "My name's Janie. My husband and I just moved in across the street." "Martha's house," the woman answered. Janie remembered seeing the name Martha Norton on the lawyer papers. "Martha Norton," Janie asked. "Yes," the old woman answered.

"My name's Peggy. Martha and I are, er...were friends. I don't get to see her anymore. She had to go to the *home,*" she added, a mournful tone in her voice. *Home.* Such a comforting word, Janie thought. But not the way Peggy said it. She knew at once what home meant for this old woman, leaning against the stair railing to help her keep her balance.

"I am sorry, Peggy. I didn't mean to disturb you. It's just...well, do you own a dog?" "A dog," chuckled Peggy. "I don't think Max and Muffin would like that very much. Peering through the screen door, Janie could see four feline eyes peering at her, curiosity filling their furry faces.

"Oh," Janie smiled. "Do you know anyone around here who does?" "No, can't say I do, but I don't get out much." Then, with a wistfulness in her eyes, she continued. "Martha had a dog, a little black Scottie named Bobby. He was the cutest thing. It broke Peggy's heart when he ran across the street and got hit by a car. I felt so bad, I think he was coming to say hello to me," she added, her eyes filling with tears. "Martha just gave up after that. She stopped eating, taking her medications. Finally, her family came to take her to that home." Janie said goodbye, feeling pretty awful for bringing such sad memories back to the kind woman.

That night, Ethan asked if she had found out anything about their nightly intruder. Janie told him about Peggy. "I feel so bad. I think I am going to bake one of my coffee cakes tomorrow and bring it over to her." "I hope you plan on baking two," Ethan said jestfully.

That night started out peacefully, but then, at about two in the morning, the barking began. This time it was more fervent, more high-pitched, filling the air with an atmosphere of excitement. Both Janie and Ethan got up and went to the back door. "Don't turn on the light," Janie said. "You don't want to frighten him away. Let's try to catch a good look at him." Together, they both waited, their eyes slowly adjusting to the moonlit yard.

"Look!" Janie cried. "Can you see him!" Ethan turned to the direction Janie pointed and saw a tiny black shadow, paws high in the air, barking and yelping with excitement. Then, the couple saw a larger shadow, a misty white figure with arms outstretched coming slowly toward him, scooping him up in her arms. The barking stopped, and the two shadows just seemed to evaporate into thin air.

Janie and Ethan didn't go back to bed. This time, no barking disturbed them, just a mix of confusion and amazement at the sight they had beheld. "I have to do something to take my mind off of what we saw," Janie muttered as the sun's first rays broke over the horizon. "Well, you did mention something about a coffeecake?" replied her sleep deprived but hungry husband.

Janie smiled, lifting some of the tenseness that had filled the night. She took out her mixer and began measuring out the flour. By the time Ethan left for work, the cake had been cooling on her kitchen counter. She wrapped it in a dishtowel and gathered up the courage to once again ring her neighbor's bell.

• • •

This time, Peggy didn't answer as quickly. Janie was just about to walk back home when the old woman opened the door, her eyes swollen and red from crying. "Peggy, what's wrong?" Janie asked. "Is it Max or Muffin?" "No," replied the old woman. "Martha's son called me this morning. She passed away during the night."

"Can I come inside?" Janie asked, extending the towel wrapped cake with outstretched arms. At Peggy's kitchen table, she began telling her friend what had happened in the darkness of her yard. At first, she worried how Peggy would react. But Peggy's face lit up with happiness. "How she loved Bobby! I am so glad she found him," she told Janie. "Thank you for telling me. You don't know how much this means to me."

Janie and Ethan never heard Bobby bark again. But now, little barks of a tiny black Scottie can be heard as he runs through the yard of a modest blue bungalow. "Shadow, time to come in," the young woman lovingly calls from her back door.

SNOW GHOST

Once upon a time, a blizzard of snow fell to the earth, thicker and softer than any before. Billions of snowflakes danced and whirled about, laughing and twirling with such glee that all the fairies in the land laughed.

"I wish this snow could last forever," said one of the little fairy children as she cupped a snowflake in her tiny hands. "You must never make a wish without much, much thought!" cried her mother. "Wishes are powerful things; we must use our gifts wisely!" she told her child, who now sat with glistening eyes that shone like the melting snow in the sunlight.

"I am sorry, mama," cried the little fairy. "I just wanted the snow to last forever." "Snow cannot last forever," her mother answered. "Each season has its time on the earth, just like we do. One day, all of us—the snow, the fairies, the trees—will all become spirits that surround us with their energy and gifts."

The little fairy had not grown into her gifts yet; they were there, but weak. She was just learning to create magick in the land. She had so much to learn, and with tired yawns, she snuggled into her little moss-lined bed and lay her head upon her lavender-filled pillow. "Good night, my child," her mama whispered as she kissed the little child's cheek.

The morning sun brought warm temperatures; the mounds of snow were disappearing as the daylight hours passed. Soon, each snowflake saw his spirit family around him, beckoning him to enter the sunbeams. All crossed into the beams and transformed into spirits, filling the air with magickal energy that nourished all living things. The trees absorbed the warm energy, the rocks and cairns breathed in its heat. The sleeping earth stirred to awaken again as the beams filled the ground.

All except one little snowflake...the snowflake the fairy child had cupped within her hands. He could not cross into the beams of light. He could not melt. "What is wrong with me?" he cried to his spirit family. "I am so cold. The light does not warm me!"

The little snowflake tried and tried to join his family. They held out their pointy arms to grasp his, but a layer of cold surrounded him and kept them back. The little snowflake cried icicles that fell to the ground where he lay. Try as he might, his cold heart could not melt. His tiny arms could not stretch to reach out to his family who were disappearing in the light. "Wait for me!" he cried. "Please don't leave me alone!" But what could they do? It was their time to leave; they had to go. "We will stay nearby, little one," his family cried. "You will feel us; we will never leave you alone." With those words, the snowflake spirits vanished into the air. The little snowflake sat, sobbing puddles of icicles in the warm, spring sunlight.

Soon, a little bird flew by. She stopped to peck at a patch of earth and drink from the puddle when she saw him. "Who are you?" she chirped, ruffling her feathers at the cold blast of air that surrounded him. "Do you know how to reach the sunbeams?" the little snowflake asked. "Why, you just spread your wings and fly," the little bird answered. And with that, she flew into the sky.

The little snowflake tried to stretch his pointy arms, but the cold, fragile points started cracking. Sadly, he collapsed into a ball of snow again and cried. Soon, a family of mice came by, searching for newly sprouted seeds. They came upon the frozen ball and sniffed and licked it. "Hey!" cried the snowflake. The startled mice jumped back and squeaked in fright. "Can you help me?" asked the snowflake. "Do you know how to reach the sunbeams?"

The family of mice shook their heads. "We like the shadows; we hide amongst the leaves and the twigs. The sunlight feels warm and nice, but it is dangerous. Others might see us and eat us!" they cried. "Eat us?" cried the snowflake. He hadn't thought about dangers. Now his mind raced with all kinds of terrors. "Oh, mama, papa, please help me!" he cried, watching the family of mice scurry on.

The little flake could not see them, but he felt a breeze of warmth surround him. It felt comforting, but still he could not melt. "Oh, mama," he sobbed. "Do not worry, my son, let magick find you again," he heard whispered in reply.

"Magick, why did that word sound so familiar?" the little snowflake wondered aloud to himself. Then, he remembered her. Her warm hands holding him in her palms, telling him she wished he could stay forever. Her hands had felt so nice, so loving. Then he remembered her hands being whisked away by another, a larger being with a harsher voice, warning her of dangers. Yes, he remembered now. *Be careful about wishes.* That's what the larger being had said.

Wishes, he thought to himself. A wish did this to me. I will wish to find the sunbeams. The little snowflake wished and wished and wished until his tired, cold body could wish no more. He fell asleep on the frozen patch of icicles that shone like a solitary diamond in the last beams of sunlight of the day.

Dusk came. This was fairy time. Fairy families were preparing for a feast, for this was a day to celebrate. The beginning of spring! Tonight would herald a fairy gathering in the moonlight, underneath the ancient trees. On such special occasions, all the woodland creatures were extended invitations as well.

Gathered inside the fairy circle, the children sat and listened to the stories of their elders. Beings of the forest were invited to tell magickal tales, as well. Little Bird chirped loudly to the children. "I have a magickal story to share," he tweeted. "I met a cold creature today, with pointy arms and tears made of icicles," he continued. "He asked me how to find the sunbeams."

"Hey, we met that strange creature too," squeaked the mice. The fairy children's eyes were wide as the circle of moonlight in the night sky. The fairy parents gathered round the mice, listening with wonder, as well. "We licked him," cried the mice. "He was cold as the winter snow, colder, and he asked us where to find the sunbeams," they added. Everyone sat, mesmerized by every word, everyone except one mother fairy whose mind wandered back to a previous afternoon and a worrisome wish.

Even fairies grow tired. Soon, the gathering was ended, and the fairies gathered up their children and headed for home. "Let's take a little shortcut," mama fairy told her child. "Why, mama? I am so tired. I want to go home."

"We may have something very, very important to do," mama answered. "Remember what I told you about making wishes? One of your wishes may have hurt someone, and that someone needs our help to change things back to the way they should be. Do you understand?" Sleepily, the tiny fairy child nodded, still a bit confused and fearing she was in trouble again.

Soon, mother and child came to the spot where they had been walking in the snow the previous day. A shimmer of light caught the child's eye. "Mama, look! It's my snowflake." Happily, the child lifted the pointed being up in her warm hands. He felt so cold; her hands felt sharp, biting pains as she held him.

"Magick," mama sighed. The little snowflake opened his eyes upon hearing that word. "Please help me!" he cried. He sobbed loudly, but no icicles fell. He had no more tears within him; he had cried them all away.

• • •

Dawn was coming; the morning sun was peeking over the horizon. "Now you must wish for him to find his sunbeam," the mama fairy told her child. "Snowflakes cannot last forever. They have a season to be, just like we do. We cannot use our gifts to change things that should not be changed. Do you understand?" "Yes, mama," the fairy child replied in a tired voice. "I am sorry," she whispered to the snowflake. "I only wanted to keep you forever because I loved you so much. I wish that you find your sunbeam."

The tiny snowflake smiled. He felt his chest warm, he felt his pointy arms soften and stretch out. He felt a warm breeze surround him and carry him into the air. He saw them waiting, his mama and papa, his sisters and brothers. They were smiling and waving their pointy arms and calling out to him. He flew toward the light and felt the warm beams envelop him. Then he was gone.

The little fairy sat, crying on the ground. Suddenly, a warm breeze flew by her wings. She thought she felt a tiny warm pinprick on her arm. "It felt like a tiny pointed arm," she whispered to her mama. Her mama smiled. "Let's go home," she whispered, scooping the little fairy child up within her arms.

Feral

Jayne Hawkings was sixty three. Not old by today's standards, but old enough to retire and find a life she had worked over forty years in achieving. She wanted a quiet little place, just large enough for her books, her collections of knickknacks...treasures only to her eyes. She wanted a little yard in which to grow things—apartment living only offered tiny window gardens. She wanted a pet, perhaps a cat or two, companions to curl up beside on wintry nights under the blankets.

Jayne scoured the listings, read the 'For Sale' ads in the newspapers. Finding nothing, she hired a real estate agent, Fran Tomkins, who covered the area that had always caught her eye and dreams. "Prices are very expensive here, you know," the realtor had cautioned. "I know," said Jayne disheartened. "Still, it doesn't hurt to look, does it?" she asked hopefully.

"There is one house," the realtor replied. "People don't want to live there because it backs up to a cemetery. Spooks my clients out, the thought of living next to dead people." "Can I see it?" Jayne asked. The quiet of a cemetery sounded just fine to Jayne after her days on Fifth Avenue, amidst the taxis and sirens and bustle of the city.

"Okay, I will set things up. We can probably go anytime. The place is vacant," Fran answered. Silently, she thought to herself, *Maybe I will finally get this dump off my hands.*

The next day, Jayne and Fran drove out to 12 Hillcrest Drive. Very few homes dotted the surrounding blocks; the neighborhood was in need of some TLC, to say the least. There it stood, downtrodden and dejected, the old blue cottage that sure enough called Oak View Cemetery her neighbor.

"Still want to go inside?" asked Fran. "It gets pretty lonely out here. Only the dead for company and a colony of feral cats that call the neglected cemetery home." Jayne was looking at the large backyard, a tangled mass of weeds and thistles. She sighed quietly to herself. This was what she wanted after all. A garden to call her own. It was just growing weeds right now, but with a little love, it could grow flowers. Why not? "Yes," answered Jayne.

The inside was lonely, longing for a friend, just like Jayne. It had a nice sized kitchen, a good thing since Jayne loved to cook. It had rows and rows of shelves along the wall in the living room, plenty of room for Jayne's collection. It had sturdy hardwood floors, and its walls were the kind built before cheap shortcuts in building materials replaced the strength of ancient trees.

"I will take it," Jayne said. "Don't you want to get a home inspector in before you make a decision?" Fran asked. "I will sign the papers today," Jayne replied. Amazed, the realtor phoned her home office to get the proper papers in order. "It's an estate, so it should be a quick closing," she added.

In less than two weeks, Jayne had hired a work crew to paint and clean and get the place livable. It wasn't the Taj Mahal, but the place certainly looked a thousand times better than when she had first stepped inside. In three weeks, she was calling it home. Jayne hired a moving company to pack up all her books and treasures.

Now, the garden. It was late spring; planting season had already begun. Jayne would have to work quickly. She didn't get up so quickly anymore when bending over, but she was determined. Little by little, the thistles were pulled, the weeds cleared. Jayne bought plants at the nearby nursery and planted them.

One day, she decided to take a stroll through Oak View. Seeing all the neglected graves saddened her. She tried pulling a few weeds, but the job was too much for her. Then, she saw a pair of yellow eyes attached to a pretty grey head studying her from behind a gravestone. "Hello!" Jayne called. The head peeking out quickly disappeared. In the distance, Jayne saw the grey shape running toward a few friends. There was a large black and white tuxedo cat, a petite calico, and a thin ginger cat by the cemetery fence.

"Oh," said Jayne. "I will have to do something about putting some fat on your bones." She went to the store, bought several bags of cat kibble (and some moist canned food for those whose teeth no doubt were in sorry shape), and went to the checkout. "How many cats do you have?" the clerk asked. "None," replied Jayne. The clerk looked at her suspiciously. Jayne didn't notice—she was on a mission.

She placed the food by the fence that backed up to her property and watched from her house. No one came. Night fell. Jayne went to sleep. The next morning, the plates were empty. Jayne smiled.

She went outside and filled them again. That's when she saw the same little grey head peeking out from behind a tree at her. "Why, hello again!" she called. Once again, the little grey head quickly darted away in the bushes. "One day," Jayne sighed.

Each day, Jayne filled the bowls. Soon, the ferals were waiting for her, though the little grey one never joined the group. Sad, because he was her favorite. She hoped upon hope that enough food was always left for him.

All that spring and summer, Jayne cared for them. That winter, she placed bins outside to shelter them. No one visited the cemetery, so no one complained. The next spring, and the next and the next for many, many seasons to pass, Jayne cared for her cats.

One autumn day, Jayne was carrying a heavy bag of kibble to the fence when she saw the grey cat. She had sadly seen many of the colony pass with the years, but this grey cat always looked the same. "Hi there," Jayne smiled. The grey cat inched closer and closer to Jayne and lifted his paw to her. Jayne reached for it and felt a feeling of love surround her like none she had ever experienced before.

Jayne's body wasn't found until the next day, when the mail lady saw her side door open and knew something was wrong. "Massive stroke...she didn't suffer," the real estate agent told the folks looking at the property. "She died in the cemetery?" they asked squeamishly. "Can we see the next house?" they asked.

Yes, Jayne died in the cemetery. Her great niece decided to lay her body at rest there, at this place she loved so dearly. There, among the weeds and tall grass, a newer stone stands. Next to it, a crumbling grey stone with a faded photograph of an old woman holding a little grey cat can be seen...if one stops and looks closely enough at the engraving.

POEMS aNd ArtWork

Rocks Amid the Stones

Headless Angels
Deflated balloons
Shriveled roses
Mold ridden teddy bears

Tokens of life
For all we amass
Collect
Treasure
Becomes
Shriveled
Moldy
Deflated
Above the earth
As our bodies
Become
Shriveled
Moldy
Deflated
Beneath

So leave a rock
Atop the headstone
Rocks are eternal
As old as the earth
Leave a token
That is endless
In hope
The body beneath
Is endless as well..........

• • •

Cemetery Winds

Fragile lives
We are born to become spirit
The cemetery winds follow
Gentle
Lilting
Lullaby breezes
Never a concern
Life has just begun
The years are long
Then increasing gusts........
The death of a parent
A close friend
A dog
The years are fleeting
The gusts settle down
Busy lives have not the time to feel
But they are there.........
Following
Watching
Unexpected
Storms of illness
Heavy gales
Lives tossed about
The years are not limitless
Time is short
Soon.........
The gentle breezes return
A whisper of air
A pass of breath across one's hair
The touch of a departed mother's hand

The glimpse of a dear dog's shadow on the floor
Gentle breezes
Waiting to lift our souls away
Gentle
Lilting.........
From whence we came
And now must return

Ghost

When hurts of mortal form are done
For those on earth whose tears are spent
Do promises of light and love
Soothe a weary spirit's heart?
Hope's light was snuffed too many times
To wish for endless flames
Perhaps to drift alone
Unseen
Untouched
Unhurt
Is light enough for some
When mortal form is done?
When decades of such tunneled grief
Lie shrouded in one's soul?
No light that flickers
Offers solace of a destination
Free
Much safer to be
Chained
On earth
Unseen
Untouched
Unhurt
Than place one's heart to trust
Another end...
To endings all the same.
Better yet to have no ending
To continue
Endless
Unseen

• • •

Untouched
Unhurt
For eternity………